U0131396

IN VISHNU'S DREAM

by Chiang Yomei

For all my teachers

IN VISHNU'S DREAM
Content

KOAN

When light strikes the point of reflection,
everything falls into place:
you and I are no more,
there is only one space,
loose yet confined,
empty yet full.

I am that space
as are you.
We are the same event.

Together
we are a trillion particles of goldness
reflecting one another;
shimmering in our nakedness,
meeting and parting,
forever counter-transmuting.

FAINA

I lay a wreath of memories
on my grandmother's nameless grave

A handful of ashes
remains of the pyre
suspended between appearances
parentheses of history

A once full life
abbreviated
to a footnote
unremarked upon
except in passing reference,
in quiet submission

to his compelling legacy

Some call it virtue,
others a waste;
I call it Love,
as I lay a wreath of papyrus-thin memories
on my grandmother's nameless grave.

IN THIS DESERTED
PART OF YOUR HEART

In this deserted part of your heart
I will wait for you

You must descend as I have
into these shadowlands

We shall meet at the familiar place
and ascend together
like new born phoenixes
toward the sun

In an instant
we will know everything
for in the falling we were born
of each other
to be two yet One -
all mysteries undone.

LONG AGO TOMORROW

Long ago tomorrow
a memory came to stay:
formless
weightless
poised for flight

Let it go
let it all go I say
for long ago tomorrow
doesn't exist today

PILGRIM

From the first step:
I hold my mind.
Looking into the flames:
I lose my mind.
Sweeping up the ashes,
I find Your Mind.

DEATH

Death
wild-eyed
ran across the page
found itself
sitting in the same position
laughing

MOTHER

Last night I dreamt of her
sitting there
looking like a china doll

I had no doubt
she smiled at some point
if not from her lips
then from her heart

My mother died
and went away
Sometimes
its as if she's never been
sometimes
its as if she's never left at all

AUTUMN

I shall think of you
when leaves begin to fall;
the season
shedding its tears
waiting
for winter to call

What have we here:
a bird
a flash across the sky
leaving no tangible trace,
like a dream.

WOMB OF DESIRE

The anatomy of loss
is a skeleton of dreams;
phantom images
with nowhere to go
stuck
in the labyrinth of hope

Still waiting,
still wanting.

Hope and fear:
forever twinned in the womb of desire.

MANDALA

From the point of view of autumn:
the harsh blade of winter
cuts mercilessly into its fragile heart
littering the earth
with the season's bones

From the point of view of winter:
it no longer boasts the easy innocence of spring

Yet the seasons wash into one another
with knowing grace;
they become one sacred wave,
rising like a serpent into the sky,
ready to swallow itself
to be renewed
again and again

SHANTI

From the hollow depths of Parsifal's dream,
broken shadows ride high on Halcyon wings

Suddenly a flash:
the moon and sun embrace;
all I can see
is sapphire ablaze

Kingfisher,
midnight's jewel,
alights a chariot of stars
gliding effortlessly onto the wish-fulfilling tree
A sadhu in disguise

We have met before
he says,
can you not remember -
in a land untouched by desire

Kingfisher,
lapis dust
fallen from the sky

Fisher King's ashes
seals a silent blessing on my heart

Echoing all around me:
Shanti
Shanti
Shanti

STARDUST

Stardust
Ash
Your breath
mine

Everything
and nothing
All Mind

Changelings
you and I
always in motion
briefly interlocking
always in the process of becoming

MY FATHER'S DREAMS

In the mirror
I see my father's dreams
gently bleeding into mine

Texture of broken grass
muted cries
imprisoned
in a house of glass

Images wrap around me
Sentiment
uninvited
as unwelcome as this humid summer rain

Father of mine
hostage of oblivion

lost in a haze of promised delights
reeking of a million what-ifs,
a cloudy concoction of sweat and compromised
scent
like an old tart's cloak
at once revolting and intriguing

The cloak casts a spell:
I struggle,
unfulfilled,
in my dream

My father's dreams
fold into my grandfather's face.
Shrouded by his own dreams
my grandfather's eyes are still on fire
wondering how it could have been

In the mirror
I see my dreams
which I do not own:
The bones of desire
which link us all
will become earth,
and dreams nothing but ashes
lighter
than a falcon's feather.

ON BEDRUTHERAN STEPS

Salt
in the air
at the tip of my tongue -

Sand
slipping through liquid fingers
freed from the texture of time

Stones
cleansed by the sea
white and cool to the touch

My face
in the wind
by the sea -

Salt in the sea
salt in my eyes
exchanging secrets

AS INSUBSTANTIAL
AS MY THOUGHTS

The wind has carried my words away
ghost-words -
thought-ashes in flight

Left unguarded,
words will chase after an echo;
an echo of an echo -
until all echoes merge with one another
and explode
toward the beginning
into itself
into an impalpable silence

BRIEFLY, IN-BETWEEN DREAMS

Shadows of the last dream
burnt to ashes by a rain of fire -
the sun
has washed away its embers

Images disintegrate
vanish and are reborn
immaculate
without the stain of sentiment

It lasts but a second,
this clarity -
the next dream
has already ensnared me.

GREAT WHITE SILENCE

Temple without walls
without the architecture of thoughts
of words
of self

White Silence
continually expanding
undoing itself
merging with the whole

No longer an idea
but an instrument of resurrection

THE EYES OF KALI

The faceless eyes of Kali
dance across the earth like mirrors

Scorching all
with the flame of time

stones rivers mountains sun moon trees skin
hair and bones

Kali
dances upon a world that is dust
breathes another world into existence
only to return it to dust

DEATH OF ME

Having lost my shadow
Weightless
I walk across this page
and dissolve
into silence
like invisible ink

ONE SEPTEMBER MORNING
MY MOTHER

Undone by time

your face

touches the periphery of my existence

Featureless

but I know it's you,

an angel,

weightless,

suffused with love and sadness

An icon

caught between two worlds

I am crossing
to the other shore
leaving you again
watching after me
with the weight of man's folly in your eyes

CORDOVA

Time
marks each stone
saying 'I am still here',
even when you become ash
I will still be here

Counting the seasons
with each passing breath
each turn of night and day
I am still here
scarring
eroding
disassembling

until everything tastes like dust
becomes dust
and night no longer unveils itself
to become day

SECRET FIRE

Shiva's dance scorches the earth,
fire-lotus ablaze
on clouds of saffron dust

Turning and turning
he picks up speed;
a thousand faces born of dust
swirl and rise up into the sky,
enveloping desires,
consuming worlds,
burning away time

Shiva's eyes meet mine;
four flames become one.

Nothing but blinding whiteness,
not even a hint of my old shadow -
only the dance,
and the white white heat
undoing all the ties that bind

LILITH SPEAKS

Lilith's veins
lead to Miriam's well;
this darkness heals.

Rage
no longer contained,
courses through her being
ripping apart seams
of carefully mended wounds.

No more tip-toeing;
Lilith says it all.

Through the fresh tear
of the ancient cut
I see myself
embedded between flesh and blood;
in shards of mirrors cracked
lay the ruins of her restless soul.

Lilith cries in pain.
Salt in her tears
renews the stagnant blood;
nourished,
it flows again.

She emerges,
a queen,
a link to our shared past,
our future.
Lilith is born again;
she is seen.

A SPACE ELSEWHERE

All around me
suspended by a pause:
white noise
white silence
just a transition

Hovering between realities
I have never been more alive
in a world stripped of identities
of definitions
of everything finite

MATTER

Virgin matter:
it exists only between lines
drawn between breaths -

When the lines soften,
begin to shiver
in their nakedness
and disappear altogether,
then there is neither breath,
nor no-breath

Virgin matter
is only an idea in your mind

Everything is recycled,
even thoughts -
nothing is original:
a new-born's cries
echo a dying man's last gasp

How final is death?
No more so than melting ice
waiting to form again
when conditions are ripe

Form
is nothing
and everything
in your mind.

INTIMATE IMMENSITY

Open the world
with your secret eye;
return to the place
before you began dreaming -

Before thoughts
before images
before the dramas took hold;
before 'I' and 'mine',
before 'action',
before Act One,
and even before the Prologue

There is a vast world beyond all this -
unexplored -
immense yet intimate,
another country
where your spirit can soar

Open the world
with your heart
and surrender completely -
fear will become a distant memory,
anger, grief and hatred
no longer a part of your anatomy

Return to the place
before you began dreaming,
before the story began,
before the seasons had meaning;
before we lost the gift of sight,
before we began dreaming.

THE HALF-MOON'S GAZE

The half-moon's gaze
is far from uncertain;
it puts pressure on time
to deliver -
something.

THE DANCE

Kali and Shiva are One,
dancing the Dance of Death,
death of death,
death of all illusions

Black Kali,
white Shiva:
pure chaos and perfect order.
Fire and ice,
night and day,
manifested yet unseen.

They dance the dance of the death of time,
burning away impurities
born of our own restless minds.

ANOTHER COUNTRY

In this briefest of encounters
between darkness and light,
a new land stirs.

This is hallowed ground,
this liquid expanse of grey -
the dreamer caught in mid-flight,
riding a chariot of sparkling embers,
suspended between night and day -

Such a tender space -
empty yet full.
Soon there will be nothing to hold onto
soon
the dreamer will disappear too

IN A MORAVIAN CEMETARY

Trees reaching for the sky like flames -
spring will still be like this
long after I'm gone

These cool smooth stones beneath my feet
marked only by time,
are silent -
holding onto an open secret
like a wound that refuses to heal

We are all transient:
like the wind
like the trees and the stones,
each breath a mirror to eternity.

THE LANGUAGE OF THE HEART

For Evie and Andy

The heart speaks a wordless verse
heard only by those
brave enough to pause,
to lift its layered veils,
follow the echoes
of an ageless rhythm
and dance
to its soundless tune

A moment ago,

forever -

a length of breath like a living temple,

liquid light,

held God-like

in the briefest glance

between two lovers

UNTITLED

Apricot buds
unfurl their dreaming hearts

velvet perfection

Perfect in bloom
perfection as they wither and fall
Immaculate

舒讀網「碼」上看

235-62

新北市中和區中正路800號13樓之3

印刻文學生活雜誌出版有限公司　收

讀者服務部

廣　告　回　信
板橋郵局登記證
板橋廣字第83號
免　貼　郵　票

姓名：＿＿＿＿＿＿＿＿＿＿　　性別：□男　□女

郵遞區號：＿＿＿＿＿＿＿＿

地址：＿＿＿＿＿＿＿＿＿＿＿＿＿＿＿＿

電話：（日）＿＿＿＿＿＿　　（夜）＿＿＿＿＿＿

傳真：＿＿＿＿＿＿＿＿＿＿

e-mail：＿＿＿＿＿＿＿＿＿＿＿＿＿＿＿

INK

INK PUBLISHING 讀者服務卡

您買的書是：_____

生日：　　　年　　　月　　　日

學歷：□國中　　□高中　　□大專　　□研究所（含以上）

職業：□學生　　□軍警公教　□服務業

　　　□工　　　□商　　　□大眾傳播

　　　□SOHO族　　　□學生　　□其他_____

購書方式：□門市_____書店　□網路書店　□親友贈送　□其他_____

購書原因：□題材吸引　□價格實在　□力挺作者　□設計新穎

　　　　　□就愛印刻　□其他_____（可複選）

購買日期：_____年_____月_____日

你從哪裡得知本書：□書店　□報紙　□雜誌　□網路　□親友介紹

　　　　　　　　　□DM傳單　□廣播　□電視　□其他

你對本書的評價：（請填代號　1.非常滿意　2.滿意　3.普通　4.不滿意）

　　　　　　書名_____　內容_____封面設計_____版面設計_____

讀完本書後您覺得：

1.□非常喜歡　2.□喜歡　3.□普通　4.□不喜歡　5.□非常不喜歡

您對於本書建議：

_____

感謝您的惠顧，為了提供更好的服務，請填妥各欄資料，將讀者服務卡直接寄或傳真本社，歡迎加入「印刻文學臉書粉絲專頁」：http://www.facebook.com/YinKeWenXue 和舒讀網（http://www.sudu.cc），我們將隨時提供最新的出版活動等相關訊息與購書優惠。

讀者服務專線：（02）2228-1626　讀者傳真專線：（02）2228-1598

浮生記行

蔣友梅

蔣友梅畫作 | 現象 · PHENOMENA

浮生記行

目次

很久以前明天

輕飄飄的往憶
恬然潛步而來
不速之客
誰知逗留多久

別刻意留它，
放了吧——
很久以前明天
都不在當下

獻給芳良

在祖母無名的墳前
獻上一環纖細的回憶

思幻
蝶影般
輕巧無情的在虛實間起舞
涸白的骨灰
懸浮在歷史和真相間

石棺是黑冰
親愛的阿娘
凍裂的笑容
已無聲

曾經

多少風韻和衷情

曾經也有理想

一生的愛憎憂懼

活潑和幽默

被修剪成短短一行歷史腳註

失落在「經國先生」輝煌的格局中

有人說

她生前的沉默是女德

有人說多麼可悲

我說這是一封沒有句點的情書

在你心中最
淒寥
的角落

我在你心中最淒寥的角落等著你
你必須
和我一樣
降身昏黑的幽影王國
尋源
讓我們在舊地重圓
如對新生鳳凰
仰噉雙飛翼——
霎時
一切了然：
在隕落時我們開始更生
二體一心
千古玄奧
都解透了

深秋

在深秋
樹落淚的時節
我總想到妳

抬頭
一隻小鳥
滑天而過
即刻無影無蹤
如夢一場

母親

昨夜我夢到她
靜靜端坐在那兒
像一個瓷娃娃

我確定
她在某個時間
曾對我會心微笑

母親過世了
離開我了

有時候
好像她未曾留連
有時候
好像她不曾告別

香客

客塵紛飛，
把持住心：
穿梭熊熊火海
徹底燒燬一切

在最絕望的當口
掃開餘燼；
哪料到
一股蓮香
清馨撲鼻

死神

目光狂妄的死神
飛沙走石
龍捲風般
掠過畫面；
意外的發現自己
端坐在起點
大笑

慾念

慾望的殘骸
失落在希望的迷宮中
無家可歸的魅影
不知何去何從

無止境的期盼
無止境的憂失：
希望和恐懼
終究是對孿生胎。

四季曼陀羅

從秋的觀點來看，
凜冬的利刃
無情地劃破它殘弱的身軀

不知道冬
是否也渴望春的撫慰？

儘管如是，
季節無罅流轉
了然優雅
匯成一堵浪波，
如巨蟒聳入天際，

回程中將自己吞噬，

再再還原，

再再重生。

曼陀羅（Mandala）：源自梵文，歷史淵遠流長，本為印、佛兩教常用名詞，意指「中心」、「圓圈」。

神翠鳥的凝視

在帕斯弗蜿蜒的夢穴中，
窺見往日殘影繽紛；
恍惚憶起：
那曾是一段太平的歲月

一片湛藍。
眨眼一眩，
日月交輝——
天呼地應，
突然間，

借搭星河列車，
青碧閃爍的神翠鳥
午夜的寶藏——

悄悄登上如意樹——

羽翼聖賢——

我們似曾相識

它炯炯的眼神

一劍射到我心底

默默地問：

「可曾記得，那片尚未被幻霧籠罩的淨土？」

神翠鳥；

默默綴地的天清遺塵——

原來是漁王的灰燼，

意外沾上了我的額頭

靜靜的賜恩。

十面八方不停迴響：

「SHANTI

SHANTI

SHANTI」

神翠鳥：希臘神話中的一種鳥，人們認為它即是翡翠鳥（Kingfisher）。據說當牠冬天期間在海邊築巢時，具有平息風浪，帶來寧靜的力量。

帕西弗（Parsifal）：帕西弗就是傳說中的「聖杯騎士」。Parsifal 在波斯文原意是「純真的愚人」Fal Parsi（Pure Fool）。在《英雄的旅程》(*The Hero's Journey*) 一書中，坎伯（Joseph Campbell）說：「我認為帕西弗是西方英雄中的佼佼者。從他身上，我們看到的是一個超越我執、向慈悲敞開自己的榜樣。」帕西弗克服重重苦難和誘惑，最後超越我執，用慈悲的力量癒合了漁王久久不治的傷口，因而尋得聖杯。「聖杯」並不一定具有宗教含義，而是超越宗教觀，隱喻人類生活中最高的精神實踐。

Shanti：Shanti 是梵文，其意為「平靜」、「安寧」。

父親的
夢

在鏡中
父親的夢
徐徐淌入我的夢
無聲的嗚咽
是禁錮在玻璃屋中的斷草殘根

感傷
有如沉悶的夏雨
凝在心窩

父親未了的夢
被酒仙拐走的夢
遍留著空望的腥氣；
像老鴇殘破失色的披肩

交雜著汗水和香水的餘味

腥臊又誘人

醉兵

魔衣的咒語

鈴鈴在耳

「一切未了」

「一切未了」

我在夢中掙扎

父親的夢

悄無聲息的疊入祖父的臉

熔入上一代未了的夢；

祖父炙熱的雙眸

仍然流露著悔憾的惆悵

叫我何時鬆口呼吸

銬住了我鼓鼓搏動的心脈

祖父的夢

鏡中

我看到

原來根本不屬於我的夢

看到

妄幻的白骨

聯結天下所有的夢

也看到

它化燼成灰

心灰夢灰

都輕於鴻毛

醉兵：作者父親蔣孝文生前的筆名。

星塵

星塵、
灰塵；
你一口氣，
我一口氣⋯
同源。

萬象、
空無，
都是念頭

你我都是蛻變兒
天地間川流不息的分子
時散時合
永遠在嬗化的過程中

We are Stardust：取自 Joni Mitchell 1969 年 "Woodstock" 一曲中的歌詞：We are stardust, billion year old carbon, we are golden.

在　海邊

鹽

浮散空中

嚐在舌尖——

看它流失於五指間

抓起一把分秒般細膩的沙石

潤滑又清涼

拾起一塊被海洗白了的石頭

海風的手

輕輕撫著我的臉頰

擦去千古的淚痕

海中的鹽

和我眼中的鹽

悄悄在交換祕密。

夢　際

初光
燎燃了昔夢餘影
燒得無燼無蹤

碎影
殂謝後再生
竟然穢痕不染

只可惜
忽來的清晰
轉瞬即逝

下一場夢
已經輕撒綱網
偷偷的誘捕了初醒的心

卡莉的雙眼

卡莉的雙眼
是時間的火炬
灼穿山河
日月
身體髮膚

卡莉
狂舞在世界的灰燼中
吐納間
又創出了另一個世界
只為了
再次將它化成灰

離　影

風

多輕易駕走了剛脫口的話；
破碎的詞語，
虛散如煙，
變成話魂

思懺
如荒原塵起
盤旋不止
盲追著自己的迴響
又追迴響的迴響
直到完全失向

回到最初始的泛世寂靜

再重新相融

相滅

在慌亂中猛撞

九月天清晨

妳的面容
隱隱徘徊在知覺邊緣
雖然
時間的沙石
模糊了妳的臉

但我知道是妳
確定是妳
無翼的天使
愛與悲愴孕育的孩子
監禁在兩個世界間
渡向彼岸
再次道別

我望著妳

望著我

妳的目光護著我

那凝視

承擔了世間千古的愚昧

科爾多瓦

光陰的故事
寫在每塊石頭上
提醒路人：
「你看，我還在」

它說：
「當你化為灰燼時，我還在。」

四季不斷交替，
日夜不息運轉，
一呼一吸間，
它說：「我仍然在」
不斷摧殘一切，
瓦解一切，

遍留瘡痕累累，
直到萬物
味同灰土，
化為灰土，
直到黑夜不再翻身變成白晝

Cordoba：也稱 Cordova，「科爾多瓦」，西班牙南部安德魯西亞的古城，古摩爾（Moorish）文化中心。

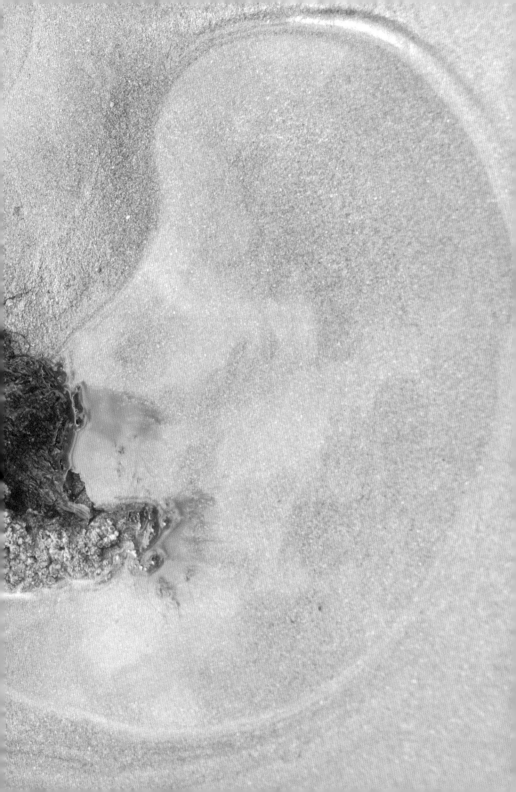

白色的寂靜

白色的寂靜
打破了思維的架構
無形的廟宇
化解了自我的定義
白色的寂靜
包融萬象
浩瀚無際
不再只是概念
而是過程

冬月的凝視

今晚弦月當空
目光炯炯
半凝視也能如此果斷
好像在追問潺潺流光
要證實什麼

另一個空間

懸浮在停留記號中
白色的噪音
和白色的寧靜
其實沒有分別

浪遊虛實間
所有的定義都化解時
多麼自在灑脫

火蓮

濕婆的舞步
灼燒大地。
朵朵火蓮盤旋向天，
一片藏紅塵雲瞬間翱起

迴旋再迴旋
舞急處千迴百轉；
千萬張臉孔
生於塵灰，
扶搖上天，
捲起世間一切慾念
燒化三千大千世界
燒化時間──

濕婆的雙眼

反映我的雙眼

四炬目光熔合成一

眩白──

三世皆空。

所有心結和桎梏都解了；

連我最後一絲昔影

都消失了

只剩下無形的舞步

和一片熾白

無我

丟失了身影，
我輕鬆地遛下頁面，
像隱形墨水
悄悄溶入寂靜中

莉莉斯如是說

莉莉斯的血脈通向瑪利亞之泉：
這黑暗可以療傷。

莉莉斯道盡一切。

不再綁手縛腳了——
割裂細細補綴的千年傷口。
像破碎的鏡片
暴流遍身，
憂憤

躺在千萬片碎鏡中的，
是她無法安息的靈魂；
我看到自己
鑲嵌在血肉之間。

莉莉斯嘶吼痛嚎。

她淚水中的鹽

活絡了凝滯已久的血，

讓它得到滋養，

再度流淌。

終於，

現身了連接過去和未來的女王——

莉莉斯不再失聲；

她復活了。

異　域

在光明與黑暗
短暫的邂逅中
一片嶄新的天地
隱隱現身：

這是一塊莊嚴的境域
一片灰色幻影
漸濃漸淡
夢者
駕著餘燼殘光
翩翩懸浮在日夜之間
柔和的空間
若隱若現

似空似實——

夢者也將無影無蹤。

再一小會兒，

就無物可依了；

再一小會兒，

大地無寸土

用你的靈目開啟全世界；
回到那夢未成形的境域中
那思慮尚未紛起，
意象尚未生根，
人生戲場尚未揭幕的境域中——
超度一切的湛寂天地。
既廣泛又微密，
那是另一個國度，
用你的心去打開世界，
徹徹底底投服於它：
恐懼將成為遙遠的記憶，
妄想情慮也不再纏身

回到一切故事發生前，

回到四季分明前，

回到分辨執著前，

回到第一場夢成形前。

光的公案

當光源射擊反光點那一剎那，
一切都明白了：
不一不異，
不生不滅——
你我是同一個空間，
同一場因緣

地水火風，
泛世萬象——
是兆萬顆金碧分子，
流轉不息，
赤裸裸的閃耀十方，
彼此相交輝映

在千變離合中，

我們不斷相互換化，

幻現幻滅。

死神之舞

卡莉和濕婆
共蹈死神之舞：
跳到死亡也死亡，
一切妄想都死亡。

黝黑的卡莉
雪白的濕婆
渾沌伴條理
冰火日夜相互交織
盤旋不止

卡莉與濕婆

二體合一

顯而不現

這舞

是超越時空的舞

能除一切苦

質地

物象本質
只存於一口氣所劃的界線間

當線條微微顫抖，
開始柔化，
再而赤裸失形時，
那口氣也消散了，
連消散的念頭都消散了

「物象本質」只不過是個概念

一切法象都是回收材料，

思維也是；

一切都是反本還原

都是過程

迴響臨終者的最後一口氣

新生兒的哭聲

死亡到底有多終極？

春雪化成水了，

到明年冬天仍會再凍結成冰

形色的虛實

只在一念之間。

在摩拉維亞墓園

有所思

在我辭世千百年後，
樹木仍會像火焰般
向太陽伸展；
春天仍舊是春天，
輪迴不息。

我腳前清涼光滑的石碑
已難見隻字，
只剩下時間留下的殘印，
不知悼念何人——

一排排枯骨般的墓碑
平躺在叢叢野草間，
默默地堅守眾所皆知的祕密，
一道拒絕癒合的傷口。

萬象轉眼即逝：

風雨沙石、你和我——

在隱隱吐納間，

每一口氣都是永恆的反映。

摩拉維亞兄弟會（The Moravian Church）：本屬西元一四〇〇年間捷克拉斯夫天主教更新運動一員；後來受迫於當地天主教，逃往德國，一七二七年岑多夫伯爵將之重組。摩拉維亞信徒去世時，安葬方式異於其他基督教徒，不是隨家族葬在同塊墳地，而是個別安葬，每個穴位上安設一塊簡單的白色平台，作為墓碑，暗喻每個人過世後在基督前是平等的。墓碑上只刻有死者姓名、生死日期和短短一句經文或是詩句。

心語

（給 Evie 和 Andy）

心所吟的詩
是無字天書
只有勇於暫停腳步的人
才能享盡它微妙的節韻
揭開層層薄紗
追隨千古的迴聲

片刻之間
永恆——
當心詩揚起時
只見一波波晶瑩流光
化成一座不朽的廟宇

若神般的定持

優雅的架在

一對情人瞬息交替的目光間

無題

杏花又開了
開的時候完美
凋謝時也完美
清純不染

浮生記行
蔣友梅

印刻文學 379

詩作・繪畫・攝影：蔣友梅
總編輯：初安民 ｜ 責任編輯：施淑清 ｜ 美術設計：空白地區Workshop ｜ 校對：施淑清、蔣友梅

發行人／張書銘 ｜ **出版**／INK印刻文學生活雜誌出版有限公司・新北市中和區建一路249號8樓・電話：02-22281626・傳真：02-22281598・e-mail：ink.book@msa.hinet.net・舒讀網 http://www.sudu.cc

法律顧問／漢廷法律事務所・劉大正律師 ｜ **總代理**／成陽出版股份有限公司・電話：03-3589000（代表號）・傳真：03-3556521・郵政劃撥：19000691 成陽出版股份有限公司 ｜ **印刷**／海王印刷事業股份有限公司 ｜ **港澳總經銷**／泛華發行代理有限公司・地址：香港筲箕灣東旺道3號星島新聞集團大廈3樓・電話：(852)27982220・傳真：(852)27965471・網址：www.gccd.com.hk ｜ 出版日期：2013年12月 初版・定價280元・ISBN 978-986-5823-54-2

國家圖書館出版品預行編目(CIP)資料

浮生記行 / 蔣友梅著. -- 初版. -- 新北市：INK印刻文學, 2013.12
（印刻文學；379）中英對照
ISBN 978-986-5823-54-2 （精裝）　　CIP 851.486 102023229

INK PUBLISHING
no.379

IN VISHNU'S DREAM

Author	Chiang Yomei
Painting&Photograph	Chiang Yomei
Chief editor	Chu An-min
Executive editor	Shih Shu-ching
Designer	Empty Quarter
Proofreader	Shih Shu-ching, Chiang Yomei

Director	Chang Shu-min
Publisher	INK Literary Monthly Publishing Ltd.
Address	8F, No.249, Jian 1st Rd., Zhonghe Dist., New Taipei City 23553, Taiwan R.O.C.
Telephone	02-22281626
Fax	02-22281598
E-mail	ink.book@msa.hinet.net
Website	http://www.sudu.cc

Legal advisor	Han Tin law office, Liu Da-zheng lawyer
Distributor	Rising Sun Publishing Co. Ltd.
Telephone	03-3589000
Fax	03-3556521
Postal transfer	19000691 Rising Sun Publishing Co. Ltd.
Printing house	Hai Wang printing Ltd.

General agent in Hong Kong & Macau Global China Circulation & Distribution Limited
Address 3/F, Sing Tao News Corporation Building, 3 Tung Wong Road, - Shau Kei Wan, Hong Kong
Telephone (852)27982220
Fax (852)27965471
Website www.gccd.com.hk

© INK Literary Monthly Publishing Ltd., 2013   CIP 851.486
PRICE 280 NTD   ISBN 978-986-5823-54-2